BOOT
CAMP

BOOT CAMP

Barbara Haley

CHRISTIAN FOCUS

© Copyright 2006 Barbara Haley

ISBN 1-84550-128-4

Published by
Christian Focus Publications Ltd,
Geanies House, Fearn, Tain, Ross-shire,
IV20 1TW, Scotland, Great Britain

www.christianfocus.com
email: info@christianfocus.com

Cover design by Danie van Straaten
Cover illustration by D Clark

Printed and bound in Denmark
by Nørhaven Paperback A/S

*As this story is set in America, American spelling
has been used throughout this book.*

Contents

Grand Prize!

"Mom! Dad!" Twelve-year-old Darin Johnson slammed the kitchen door behind him. "I'm home."

"So, what do you expect — a party?" Darin's fourteen-year-old sister, Tamara, stood at the sink rinsing dishes and loading them into the dishwasher.

Ignoring the remark, Darin tossed his Bible on the table and grabbed a cookie from the package on the counter. "Where are Mom and Dad?"

"Beats me." Tamara shrugged. "Last time I checked it wasn't my day to watch them."

"Mom?" Darin walked out of the kitchen and headed upstairs, taking the steps two at a time. "You're not going to believe this!"

"We're in here," his mother called from the study. "Dad's trying to hook up this computer. I thought you were going to phone when Scouts was over."

"The Thompsons gave me a ride," Darin said, entering the room. "Awesome!" Darin's eyes lit up as he checked out the new computer. "Do I get the old one in my room?"

Mr. Johnson smiled from where he knelt behind the computer desk. "We'll have to see about that. I'm sure Tamara has her eyes on it, too."

"But I asked first, right?" Darin argued. "That should count for something."

"Fat chance!"

Darin wheeled around to see Tamara in the doorway, her hands on her hips. "I'm three years older than you. I need it much more than you do," she said.

"I don't think so," Darin said. "All you ever do is talk on the phone. What do you need a computer for — to keep track of what you've told everyone?" Darin laughed at his own joke until he noticed no one else was laughing.

"That's enough, you two," Mr. Johnson said. "Keep it up and I'll give the thing to someone at the office."

Mrs. Johnson sat down in a blue and yellow flowered easy chair in the corner of the room. "Darin, weren't you going to tell us something when you came in?"

Puzzled, Darin glanced over at his mother. Then he remembered. "Oh, yeah! You are not going to believe what I found out tonight! You know the essay I had to write for the competition two months ago?"

Mrs. Johnson put her hand to her mouth. "Darin! You didn't..."

Darin punched the air enthusiastically. "I did! I won the wilderness trip. The Grand prize!"

"No way!" Tamara screamed. "You're lying!"

Shaking his head, Darin continued. "I get to invite two friends to go with me over spring break. Three days out in the open on our own.

11

Nobody to boss us around or tell us to quiet down." Darin's eyes were closed, a grin across his face. "Sweet!"

Darin's father laughed. "Sounds like a release from prison."

Opening his eyes, Darin blushed. "Oh. I didn't mean that it's bad around here or anything. It's just that..."

Now both of his parents were laughing. "We understand, Darin," his mother said. "Now go brush your teeth and get ready for bed. Until spring break you're still under our command."

Real funny. Darin rolled his eyes as he walked down the hall to his bedroom. Passing Tamara's room, he heard her talking on the phone to one of her friends.

"This is so not fair," she moaned. "That kid gets every lucky break. Why don't I ever win anything?"

"Maybe because all you ever do is talk about entering contests," Darin muttered. Shutting his door behind him he plopped down on the bed. Folding his arms behind his neck, he thought about which friends he would invite.

This was going to be really difficult. Of course he'd ask Andrew McGinnis, his best friend, but beyond that, he didn't know.

Rolling to his side, he watched his four goldfish swimming in the tank on his dresser. The smallest one chased a larger fish under the tunnel and behind a rock. Darin laughed. "You go, Shorty," he cheered. Swinging his legs over the edge of the bed, he stood and went to the bathroom to brush his teeth. Staring in the mirror at his dark brown curls, he imagined camouflage patches of green, brown, and black across his cheeks. *"I'll bring along some peroxide and bleach my hair. This is going to be way too cool."*

"Darin?" Tamara pounded on the bathroom door. "Hurry up. I need to go."

"I just got in here," Darin answered, wetting his fingers and pushing his hair off his forehead.

Peering in the mirror one last time he smiled to himself. *"Maybe I'll get a buzz before I go — like a real Marine. High and tight."*

Pushing his T-shirt sleeve up high into his armpit, he bent his arm and examined his muscle. Growing. Still, Darin was not satisfied. *"I have really got to get in shape. Maybe Dad will let me join the fitness center down the street."*

"Mother!" Tamara shouted, outside the door.

"I'm coming," Darin hollered. "Hold your pants on!" Opening the door slowly, he pushed past his sister, dodging to avoid her elbow.

"Darin." This time it was his father calling from downstairs. "Your mother and I want to talk to you."

"Great," he muttered. "Can't a guy even have a little extra time in the bathroom?"

"Coming," he yelled. Darin slipped into a sweat suit, grabbed a pair of socks, and headed downstairs.

Eat Your Words

Halfway down the stairs, Darin leaped to the bottom and dropped to his knees. Scurrying behind the recliner, he pulled an imaginary trigger on his rolled-up pair of socks, threw them across the room, and yelled, "Arm yourselves, men. The enemy's approaching!" Straightening his left arm, he fashioned his hand into a gun, his index finger pointed forward and his thumb raised as a scope. Leaning out from behind the chair, he swung his arm back and forth, scanning the territory in front of him, and pulled the trigger halfway down his arm. "Tuh-duh-duh-duh-duh!"

He could see his parents sitting beside each other on the sofa. *"This doesn't look good,"* he thought. *"They're together on whatever bomb they're about to drop."*

Darin crawled across the room, grabbed his socks, and plopped down in the recliner. "This is going to be so awesome! You think I can join the fitness center down the street for a month, Dad?"

Mr. Johnson grinned. "I'll look into it. They might have a trial membership available for free."

"Yes!" Darin said, pumping his arm. One out of one! He decided not to press his luck. He'd ask about the haircut another day.

"About the computer," Mrs. Johnson said. "We've decided to let Tamara have a turn first."

"What?" Darin started to jump to his feet, but common sense kicked in, and he forced himself to stay put. After all, he wouldn't get anywhere with the haircut idea if he got on mom's bad side by pitching a fit about this. She didn't seem to notice his initial reaction. Good.

"Tamara's very upset about you winning the contest."

"*So wha-a-at? Like she ever puts any effort into anything besides shopping and painting her nails? Like I should be penalized now just because I took the time to write an essay on a Saturday?*" Darin swallowed his thoughts and nodded. "I know."

Mr. Johnson stretched his arms and folded them behind his head. "You'll get your turn, Darin. I thought we could switch every three months."

"Three months?" Darin asked, his voice a bit too loud. The words slipped out before he could stop them. His dad definitely noticed.

"This isn't going to be an issue," Mr. Johnson said, sticking his open hand out to stop the argument. "Understand?"

"Yes, sir."

Darin unrolled his socks and curled his legs up into the chair. "So... is that what you called me down for?" He shoved his foot into the second sock only to discover a huge hole. Poking his big toe through, he grabbed his leg and brought his foot up to eye level. Wiggling his toe, Darin scrunched his eyebrows. "Attention!" he ordered. The toe stopped wiggling and stood straight and tall. "Hit the ground, Private! Give me fifty."

Working his toe up and down, Darin started counting. "One... two... three... Faster, you wimp! Show me some muscle!" Darin's toe flew into high speed... and then...

"Earth to Darin...Come in, Darin," Mr. Johnson said, a smile on his face.

Suddenly, Darin returned to the living room and saw his parents' faces across the battlefield. "Oh!" he said, his face going red. "Sorry — guess I'm way too excited, huh?"

"That's fine, Son," Mr. Johnson said. "But there's something else we need to talk about."

Darin slipped his feet beneath him and pulled himself up straight in the chair. This definitely didn't sound good. "Yes, Dad?"

"It's about the wilderness trip ..."

"Yes," Mom interrupted. "Your dad hasn't

heard the report you wrote. Why don't you go get it and read it to him?"

Darin saw Dad's look when Mom interrupted him. There was obviously more coming. But it could wait. Darin jumped up and ran to the kitchen to get a copy of his report. Returning to the living room, he handed the paper to his dad.

Mr. Johnson shook his head. "No. I want you to read it to me." He handed the paper back to Darin.

Slimey goosebumps starting crawling down Darin's back. "Am I... like... in trouble or something?"

"Why, no, dear," Mrs. Johnson said. "Dad just wants to hear this in your own words."

"Okay." Darin opened the paper and began reading. "Teamwork."

"Great title," Mr. Johnson said.

"They gave us that," Darin told him.

"Go ahead, dear," Mrs. Johnson whispered, her hands clasped together in front like she was about to break into prayer or something.

"Teamwork is about working or playing together. It is about learning to accept others no matter how cool or weird they might be. It is not about just choosing your friends every time you pick teams for soccer or other sports. Teamwork involves more than friendship. Teamwork requires patience and cooperation.

"The Bible talks about teamwork in Romans 15:5-7. It's Paul who is talking. He says, 'May the God who gives endurance and encouragement give you a spirit of unity among yourselves as you follow Christ Jesus, so that with one heart and mouth you may glorify the God and Father of our Lord Jesus Christ. Accept one another, then, just as Christ accepted you, in order to bring praise to God.'

So, I believe that teamwork is not only important, it is something God wants Christians to be a part of. That's why I am going to try to accept others just like God accepts me."

Darin slipped back into the recliner, folding the paper and dropped it to the floor. "So... that was it."

Mr. Johnson cleared his throat. "It was very good, Son, and it should make what we want to talk to you about easier if you really mean what you wrote," Mr. Johnson said.

"Mean what I wrote?" Darin thought to himself. "Who cares? I just wanted to win the trip. Why does everything have to be so serious around here? Why can't we just turn the lights off and play battlefield with flashlights or something?"

"You did mean what you wrote, didn't you, Darin?"

Darin realized his father was still speaking to him. "Well... sure. I mean, I guess so. Why?"

At this point, Darin saw his mother shut her eyes. "She really is praying," Darin realized. "What is going on? They act like I'm really going off to war or something. I mean... chill!"

His father sat forward on the sofa, leaned his elbows on his knees, and propped his chin on his folded hands. "Great! Another... father-to-son... talk — no, discussion." Darin sighed.

His father spoke up, "Your mother and I were talking about the trip, Darin, and we'd like you to consider... ."

"Oh, no! This is so not happening," Darin pleaded silently. "They are not going to tell me I have to invite Tamara. Oh, God. Please zap them with some wisdom... some kindness... some understanding!"

"Darin?"

"Yes, sir?"

"If you can stay with me for a moment, I'll explain."

"No way! I missed it! What did he say?" Darin knew Dad had dropped the bomb because both he and Mom were watching him like he was about to sprout wings or something. He nodded. "I'm with you, Dad."

"Okay. Well... we figured that you could really make a statement for your Christianity by inviting him — you know, like putting your best foot forward."

"Him? Best foot? Tell me what I missed. What IS he talking about?" Darin scrunched up his nose. "I have to play this right." With a puzzled look on his face, he smiled — just a little. "No overkill, here. Be cool. "

In a quiet, respectful, voice he asked, "I don't really understand, Dad. Can you tell me again?"

Now it was Mr. Johnson's turn to look puzzled. He turned to Darin's mom. "Maybe you can do a better job, honey."

Darin saw the eye contact. He loved to interpret their eyeball conversations. They were SO obvious.

Dad: The kid is nuts. What's there not to get? I give up. He's all yours.

Mom: You just have to be patient. I told you that I should be the one to bring the idea up.

Dad: So... do it! Show your stuff. Just hurry. I'm missing a game on television.

Mom: Smile. Watch.

The goosebumps had now completely taken over Darin's body. They made their way through the wax in his ear canals and even successfully invaded his boxer shorts. Darin started to scratch, but no one seemed to notice. It was all about what they had to say.

"Well... bring it on. I'm a man — a Marine. I can take it!"

You've Got to Be Kidding!

Mrs. Johnson took a few moments to prepare herself. Straightening her skirt, she folded her hands in her lap and took a deep breath.

"Okay, all ready," Darin groaned inside. *"Enough dramatics. Just spill the beans. Take the plunge. Throw the grenade. PLEEASE!"*

"Your father and I think that inviting Judd would be a perfect way to show your friends that you really have accepted him as one of the group. You know, after the trouble you had with him at the first of the year and all. Of course, Judd's family could probably never afford such a trip, but your father and I are prepared to offer to..."

"STOP!" Darin screamed, holding his hands over his ears, his eyes squeezed shut. They call it "shell-shock," don't they? Combat fatigue. A direct result of continued artillery fire. He couldn't take anymore. Judd? JUDD? Darin wondered if his parents were purposely trying to injure him. How could they even suggest such a bizarre idea? "This is the guy who made my life a misery last year. He bullied me! He really pushed me around."

"Yes, and you wrongly accused him of stealing my war medal - which you shouldn't have taken into show and tell in the first place. I'd told you NO! Your disobedience caused this family a lot of grief and..."

"But Judd's an idiot! HE'S A BIG IDIOT!"

"Darin!" Mr. Johnson said, jumping to his feet. "You are pushing the limits, young man! I'm not sure you even need to go on this trip — screaming at your mother and I like that. What on earth has come over you?"

Mrs. Johnson dissolved into tears, dabbing her eyes with that dainty little hankie she always pulled out of nowhere when she fell apart.

Darin could see the veins bulging in his father's neck and his ears twitching as he reached over and took Darin by the arm, pulling him to his feet. He could feel his father's watchful stare, though he kept his eyes glued to the floor.

"You've done it now, soldier! How dare you speak to the commanding officer's wife with such disrespect?"

No one was talking. Darin knew his father was waiting for him to explain. To apologize. Anything. He tried to think about what would be best to say. His big toe wiggled. *"Not now, Private. Don't even think about taking advantage of this situation."* The toe wiggled again, back and forth. *"Laughing at me, huh? I'll show you! I'll..."*

Darin shook his head. *"Get a grip, Darin. This is not the time!"* Looking up into his mother's face, he really did feel bad. "I'm sorry, Mom. I don't know what happened. I mean... Judd? I can't believe you're asking me to do this."

By now, Darin's body was trembling and tears threatened to shoot from his eyes like a water fountain with a fan behind it.

"Sit down," Mr. Johnson said, releasing his grip on Darin's shoulder.

At ease. Darin fought to focus. "I can't, Dad. I wouldn't have ANY fun if Judd came. You know how he likes to tease me."

"He idolizes you, Darin. You know that," Mrs. Johnson said. "This could be the opportunity of a lifetime for him. A Christian camp could be just what he needs."

"But..."

There went Dad's hand in the air again. His way of regaining the floor. Taking control. Keeping the troops in shape. "We're not telling you that you have to invite him, Darin," Mr. Johnson said softly. "It's just a suggestion."

"Right. Like I'm going to earn any points that way. Like life is going to be a great big piece of chocolate if I refuse. NOT!"

"So... I - I don't have to invite him?" Darin asked.

His mother's eyes shot open. Wide. "You don't want to?"

Where is God?

"Pray about it, Son," Mr. Johnson said as Darin grabbed his Bible and thumped his way up the stairs, his parents' words ringing in his ears. "God will show you what to do."

"*Right. Like maybe God will provide a way for me to find another family,*" he muttered, kicking the next step. "*Like maybe God will cause Judd to disintegrate right in front of my eyes... Yeah... like God's going to answer that prayer!*"

Darin was so deep into his thoughts, he practically tripped over Tamara who had positioned herself on the top step, safely behind the enemy lines, to observe the battle below. Darin didn't even care.

"This stinks!" Tamara said as he walked by. "Mom and Dad just passed an all-time high for making life miserable, huh?"

"Yeah," Darin said as he shut his bedroom door behind him. Pulling up a chair, he flipped it around and straddled it in front of his fish tank. "You've got it made, Shorty," he muttered to his goldfish. "You just swim around at leisure. No one to boss you about. No orders — just life in the fast lane."

Darin picked up the round, yellow can of fish food and flipped the lid. Sprinkling a handful across the top of the tank, he watched the fish zoom for their dinner.

"Sorry I'm late, guys. Had to sit in on some top-level negotiations... They want me to be the hit man... You know, take a fall so someone else can score."

"Who took the fall for you, Darin. On Calvary?" Darin froze. The goose bumps were back. Jesus did that. He had come to earth even though He knew He was going to be blamed for all kinds of stuff He didn't do. He also knew that He was going to be put to death.

Darin sighed. "Then there's the last part of the verse I used in my report. Romans...?"

Darin's mind went blank. He couldn't remember what the ending of the verse said.

Reaching for his Bible, he turned to Romans 15 and reread the last verse he'd quoted in his paper.

"Accept one another, then, just as Christ accepted you, in order to bring praise to God."

"Don't do it for your parents, Darin. If you decide to do it, do it for Jesus."

Darin knew that this was God speaking to him, prompting him. It was God who made him remember the Bible verse — even if he couldn't quite remember it all. It was God who brought him to think about Jesus.

He'd been told about his conscience since he was a kid - about the voice inside that God used to lead him in the right direction. But this time it was different. Darin felt that it was stronger. Jesus was in his heart, part of his life. God could communicate with him.

"This is going to be hard God." As soon as the words slipped from his mouth, Darin felt bad. "Uh... sorry, Lord. It was hard for You to die for me, right?" Then Darin realized what God was saying. "You want me to ask Judd to come to camp, to bring praise to You, God?"

A warm peace flowed Darin's body — like the feeling he got when he went camping in December and curled up in a sleeping bag. This was right. This was God.

"Thanks, God. Thanks for taking time to talk to me. How did You know I needed You right now?" Darin sat back and nodded his head. "Yes God. I know - that's who You are. You know what I need before I even ask. I can trust You. You're always with me."

Darin grinned as he looked around his room. "Okay, then," he said, his heart about a hundred pounds lighter. "I'll do this for You, Lord." He pushed his chair back under his desk, flipped the lights off, and climbed into bed. "You and me, Commander. We'll face this battle together and come out the winners!"

Surprise at Lunch

Darin shoved his books into his locker the next morning and waited for Andrew.

"Hey, Darin," Brett called.

Brett was Darin's second best friend. The one who WOULD have come along on the wilderness trip. A tiny pain poked Darin's conscience as he remembered that he was no longer doing this for his parents, but for God. "Oops. Sorry, Lord," he mumbled under his breath as Brett walked up.

"How'd you do on the science test?" Brett asked. "I bombed it big time!"

Darin hated these questions. He always aced his tests and hated to admit it to his friends. He smiled. "I bombed it, too."

"Yeah, right," Brett said, punching Darin on the arm. "Like cows can fly."

Darin looked up, shading his eyes with his hand. "Hey, that would be pretty cool, actually. We'd have to be careful, though. Cows can make some pretty big drops."

"Gross!" That came from Hannah. Her locker was right next to Darin's. "You DIDN'T just say what I thought you said."

"He did," Brett said, holding Hannah's books for her while she looked in the daisy-shaped mirror she had glued in the door of her locker and combed her hair. "He's sick, isn't he?"

"Sick, nothing!" Darin said, grabbing Hannah's books. "And what are you doing? This is my job."

Hannah blushed, but smiled. "Now, boys. Let's not fight over my books."

Darin's ears went purple. *Why do I always feel this way around Hannah?*

"Who's fighting over what?" Andrew asked as he walked up. "What did I miss?"

"Nothing, much," Brett said. "We're just going to lunch. Grilled pickles with cheese, I think." He turned and started walking toward the cafeteria. Andrew and Darin joined him. "I hear you won the grand prize at Scouts last night, Darin. Pretty cool!"

"What?" Andrew said. "How you going to tell Brett before you tell your best friend? What's up with that, Johnson?"

Darin laughed. "Pipe down, Andrew. I didn't tell Brett. My guess is that Tamara called his older sister and told her. Right?"

Brett nodded. "Exactly. So who you going to invite?"

Darin walked through the door of the cafeteria and picked up his tray and silverware. *"Okay, God. You still there? What do I do now?"*

One of the high school seniors pushed between Darin and Brett with a tray. "Picking up lunch for a teacher, kids," he said in a deep voice. "Sorry." He smirked. "Sort of."

In his mind, Darin just pushed past the guy, flicking the tray onto the cafeteria floor, leaving the Senior to pick up the mess. But, on the outside, he just moved over and let the bigger guy go by. At least now he had some time to figure out what to do about Brett and Andrew. *"Any ideas, God?"* Darin wasn't too pleased with the next thought that came to his mind. *"You could tell the truth?"* Oh, no. That was really asking a lot.

The chef plopped some sort of meat and potato casserole on his tray and handed it back to Darin. He took one look at it and grinned. "Maybe cows can fly and they've been flying in the kitchens? No, Darin. Don't even go there."

Grabbing a bottle of water, he wandered through the dining hall to one of the tables in the back.

Moments later, Brett and Andrew sat down in their assigned seats across from Darin. Andrew didn't waste any time bringing the subject up again. "So... what do you say, Darin? The three of us? That would totally rock!"

"Hey, guys! What would rock? A volcano?" Judd laughed at his joke as he sat down next to Darin, stuck out his elbows, and began shoveling food into his mouth with both hands.

"Can life get any worse?" Darin ate a mouthful of lettuce followed by a bit of the casserole to avoid answering Andrew's question. But there is only so long you can hold soggy lettuce in your mouth. Darin swallowed — twice. The lettuce refused to stay down. Choking, Darin grabbed his water and tried to force the wilted vegetable down his food track.

Judd, trying to help, of course, slapped Darin between the shoulder blades and pulled his arms above his head. That did the trick. The meat and potato, lettuce, and water combination flew from Darin's mouth, spraying Andrew's face and tray of food.

"DISGUSTING!" Andrew screamed, jumping up from the bench. "SICK!"

He grabbed every napkin in sight and wiped his face. "You big thug!" he yelled, staring at Judd. "Can't you do anything right in life?"

"What's going on here, boys?" It was Miss Poe, Darin's teacher.

She took one look at Andrew's tray and started heaving, right there in front of the class. With her mouth clamped shut and her cheeks blown out like balloons, she turned and ran for the nearest restroom.

"Awesome," Brett said. "Coolest thing to happen at school in ages."

Darin Breaks the News

Darin and Brett were on the soccer field when Andrew came outside. They burst out laughing when they saw the T-shirt the school nurse had given him to wear. It looked like it was about three sizes too big for him and had a giant S across the front. Superman would have been okay, but when you got up close, Andrew's shirt said "Somebody is Special!"

"Don't even think about saying anything," Andrew growled. "Wouldn't you know, my mom is too busy to pick me up or go get me a clean shirt."

Darin tried hard to stop laughing, finally deciding to change the subject. "Hey, let's go play tetherball. No one's over there, right now."

"Fine with me," Andrew mumbled, tagging along behind Darin and Brett.

"So... did you make any decisions while I was gone?"

Darin shook his head. "There's more to it than you know."

Andrew laughed. "Yeah, like you can't decide between me and Judd, right?" He ran ahead and grabbed the tetherball on its string and swung it around to get it going. "Come on, Darin. Tell the truth. You can't decide, right?" Andrew doubled over, he was laughing so hard by now.

Brett didn't even smile. Darin looked at him. "You know, don't you?"

Brett nodded. "It's okay. My parents have a trip to the Smokey Mountains planned. I couldn't have gone anyway."

Stopping the ball, Andrew walked over to Darin and Brett. "Wait. What are you guys talking about? What does Brett know?"

But before Darin could answer, Judd came running across the playground. "Guess I'll play with you guys. Who's choosing teams?"

Andrew walked away and sat down on a bench nearby. "I'm not playing."

Judd looked at Darin and Brett. "You guys playing?"

Brett shook his head. "I don't think so."

Judd's face dropped. He looked at the ground. "I guess I understand."

Darin felt sorry for him. No one wanted to play tetherball with Judd. He was just too strong and nearly always ended up punching the ball into some innocent kid's head. "I need to talk to you, Judd."

"Me?" He lifted his head and grinned.

"Yeah." Darin led the way over to the bench and sat down by Andrew. Judd and Brett sat down on the ground. "I was wondering if you'd want to go with Andrew and me to a wilderness camp over spring break. My parents said they would pay your way."

"Me?" Judd said — his jaw hanging. "Do you mean it?"

"Him?" Andrew said — his jaw hanging. "You really are going to invite him?"

Brett caught Darin's attention, grinned, and rolled his eyes. "Them?" he mocked in a whiney voice. "You're going to invite them?"

Darin laughed. "Yes. Judd and Andrew. And aren't we going to have fun!"

* * * * *

Andrew waited until Judd got off the bus after school to bring the subject up again. "You can't do this, Darin. We're not going to have any fun with him along."

"It's done, Andrew. If you don't want to come, I can ask someone else."

Andrew slammed his fist into the seat in front of him. "Why are you doing this? Your parents making you?"

"It was their idea, actually," Darin admitted.

"Did they force you or pull one of those 'We want you to think about this' tricks on you?"

Darin nodded. "Something like that."

"And you couldn't reason with them — make them understand?"

Hesitating, Darin decided to be honest. "I didn't try."

Andrew threw his hands in front of him, palms up, his eyes wide with disbelief. "What's up with that? You're killing me, Darin."

"It's sort of a God-thing, Andrew. I was thinking about my parents' suggestion that I invite Judd along. It's like sacrificing my own desires..." Andrew's blank face said it all. "What I mean is that what I want shouldn't be the most important thing. When I understood that I realized that Jesus sacrificed his life for me. He suffered more than I'll ever know."

Andrew jerked back in the seat and scrunched up his nose. "Jesus? Wilderness camp? Where are you going with this? I do NOT understand!"

"There's a verse in the Bible that talks about getting along and accepting each other in order to bring praise to God. I just want to do that, Andrew."

Andrew narrowed his eyes and shook his head. "Whatever, Darin."

A Quiet Ride

"Senior citizens and passengers traveling with young children may board at this time."

Mr. Johnson tapped Darin on the shoulder when the announcement came over the loudspeaker at the airport. "That's you guys."

"What?" Andrew asked. "Don't call me no baby or old wrinkly."

Judd laughed, slapping his knee. "That's a good one, Andrew."

"Shut-it, Judd," Andrew snapped. "Are you serious, Mr. Johnson?"

Darin looked at his dad — an eyeball conversation of their own.

Darin: See what I'm going to have to live with for three days?

Dad: Pretty bad, huh? You can do it, though.

Darin: Pray for me.

Dad: Sure.

"Boys?" A young man walked up to the group, wearing navy uniform shorts and a white shirt. "You ready to go?"

They nodded.

"I'm Steven, and I'll be your host for the trip today. Go ahead and grab your things and we'll get you settled before we let the general public board."

Darin picked up his backpack and hugged his dad.

"I'm proud of you, Son," Mr. Johnson whispered in his ear. "God is with you."

"*This is sort of sad. And scary.*" Darin shook it off and caught up with Andrew and Judd who were following Steven down the ramp. "Hang on, guys," he hollered.

Steven took them to the first three seats of the coach section and told them to get buckled in.

"What's up with this?" Andrew asked. "Why can't we sit in those fat people seats up front? I'd rather ride in style."

"Those are first class seats," Darin told him. "People pay extra for them."

"Rats," Andrew said. "Hey, look at all the buttons. Let's see what they do." He pushed one after another until Darin grabbed his arm.

"Grow up, Andrew," he said as he sat down in the middle seat to keep Andrew and Judd apart. Judd plopped down beside the window.

"Hey! Who says you get the best seat Dud?" Andrew asked. "Maybe I would like to be able to see out the window."

"Sorry," Judd answered. "Already got my seatbelt hooked. Better luck next time."

"Well, maybe I'll just show you how to unhook it..." Andrew said, leaning over and reaching for Judd's seatbelt.

Darin yanked his arm away. "Sit down, Andrew. You're my guest, and I say this is how we're doing it. You can have the window seat on the way home." Darin was relieved when Andrew agreed to be seated without any further complaints.

"Ladies and gentlemen," came the voice over the intercom. "I'd like to have your attention as we go over a few safety instructions." A middle-aged female attendant with curly dark brown hair stood in the aisle next to Andrew, waving her arms this way and that, pointing to different parts of the plane.

Andrew imitated everything she did, making faces all the while. By the time the announcements were finished, he had everyone in the front section in stitches — with the exception of the attendant.

"Listen, kid," she whispered, crouching low to get in Andrew's face. "You'll leave the buttons alone and read your comic if you want a snack later. Got it?"

Andrew nodded, pushing himself as far back in the seat from the attendant as he could manage. The attendant stared at Andrew one last moment, and then plastered a smile back on her face and continued down the aisle.

"Whew!" Andrew said. "That woman definitely needs a breath mint!"

Darin had been so busy watching Andrew that he didn't realize how quiet Judd had gotten as the plane taxied down the runway. Turning in Judd's direction, he immediately understood. "Push the button, Andrew. Get an attendant."

Judd was turning green, his eyes rolling to the back of his head. "O-o-h-h-h," he moaned. "I think I'm going to be sick!"

Darin found a barf bag in the pocket in front of him just as the wheels of the plane left the ground.

Judd grabbed it and hurled everything he'd had for breakfast, lunch, and part of last night's dinner in the bag. "A-a-w-w-w," he said, holding his stomach, and leaning back against the pillow behind his head. Puke stuck to his lips, and the bulging bag, tipped in his hand, seemed dangerously close to spilling all over Darin's leg.

"Push the button, Andrew!" Darin called again.

"Are you kidding?" he said. "And get dragon breath back? No way!"

Fortunately, a kind woman across the aisle rang for the attendant, and Steven came and took the bag away, returning shortly with napkins and a piece of gum.

Judd wiped his mouth and handed Steven the soiled napkins. Steven opened a second barf bag and asked Judd to place the napkins inside. As Judd did so, though, a chunk of puke fell down the front of his shirt. Looked like a piece of chicken or tuna. Darin almost gagged. He pointed it out, and Judd wiped it up, leaving just a small stain.

"I'm going to the bathroom," Andrew said, unbuckling his belt. "I can't take this smell."

"I'm sorry," Steven said, raising his eyebrows. "You're going to have to take it for now. Until the captain turns off the seat belt light, you must stay in your seat at all times."

"Whatever," Andrew mumbled, pinching his nose shut and shutting his eyes. "Let the fun begin."

Judd slept the rest of the way to Missouri.

"Seems like a waste of a good window seat,

50

if you ask me," Andrew complained a bit later in the flight.

"You want that seat, now?" Darin asked, with a grin on his face. "I'm sure Judd would be willing to trade."

"Real funny," Andrew said. "Let's play with my video game." He grabbed his bag with his feet and scooted it out from under the seat until he could reach the handle and pull the bag up onto his lap.

"Your video game?" Darin asked. "I told you not to bring that. This is supposed to be a 'Back to Nature' experience."

Andrew shrugged his shoulders. "Not until we get there." He plugged in the two controls and set the game up. "Come on, Darin. You know you want to play."

Darin Speaks Up

"Camp Wilderness — this way!" A counselor in green shorts and T-shirt stood in the middle of the hall with a sign. "Any campers?"

"Like he doesn't already know there are three boys flying in on this plane," Andrew said. "Who could miss us, anyway, with the flight attendant leading us around like a pack of dogs?"

"Darin, Judd, and Andrew?" the counselor asked as the boys approached.

They nodded. Darin stuck out his hand. "Darin Johnson, sir."

The man grabbed his hand shook it firmly. "Commander Stone, here. Welcome to St. Louis. And this is..."

"Judd Becker, sir."

Darin grinned. Judd topped the counselor by at least two inches.

"And... "

"Andrew McGinnis, sir."

"Oh!" Commander Stone jumped back a step or two when he grabbed Andrew's hand.

Darin wanted to die. *Grow up, Andrew. Leave your toys at home.*

"What you got there, Son?" the commander asked. Andrew handed him the electric shock ring he'd worn when shaking hands.

"Gets people all the time," Andrew said, laughing.

The commander wasn't smiling. "Well, it just got you K.P. duty. Six o'clock sharp. Report to the mess hall. Understood?"

"Y-yes, sir," Andrew said.

The boys were quiet on the hour-long ride through the hills to the campsite. Judd started getting sick again until the driver slowed way down. "We'll have to take the highway when we return to the airport," the commander said. "Makes for a longer trip, but there aren't so many hills."

"Thanks," Judd said, in barely a whisper.

When they got to camp, Commander Stone hauled Judd off to the sick bay and sent Darin and Andrew to the cabin to lay their bed rolls out on their cots. Supper would be in fifteen minutes.

"You think he was serious about kitchen duty?" Andrew asked as soon as he and Darin were alone.

"I don't know. I guess so. He looked pretty serious."

"Yeah, but I didn't come here to be tortured. I could have stayed home and done that."

Andrew and Darin hurried into the cabin. Most of the bunks were already taken, but Darin found three bottom bunks together near the door. "Which one do you want?" he asked Andrew. "You can have first pick."

"I don't know. Let me try them out."

"Just hurry, Andrew. Everyone else has already headed over for dinner."

"Okay, okay." Andrew threw his sleeping bag on the bed closest to the door and dug into his bag for his pillow. "Hey, Darin. You bring an extra toothbrush?"

"Nope. Don't worry, though. I don't think anyone will be checking to be sure you brush your teeth."

"Not me," Andrew said. "Judd. That boy's mouth is a regular excavation site. Ever looked inside?"

"Gross." Darin spread out his sleeping bag and then reached over to make up Judd's bed. "I hope you don't plan on ruining this trip by bugging Judd all the time."

"What? Like he doesn't drive me nuts? You know that boy's about one French-fry short of a Happy Meal!"

Darin turned, his face red. "Yeah, and so what, Andrew? Like you're so special? Should have worn your T-shirt to let everyone know!"

Andrew sat down on his bed. "Sorry, Darin," he said meekly. "What's up? You never talked to me like that before? We still friends?"

Darin shoved his bag under his bunk. "Sorry, too. I guess I've just been so uptight about this trip — with Judd coming and all. But it's you that keeps causing the trouble, Andrew. Can't you let up so we can have some fun?"

Without saying another word, Andrew walked out the door, letting it slam behind him.

Darin sat on his bed for a minute before he followed. "Are you there, God? I sure hope so because this isn't turning out so well. Please help Andrew and Judd to get along. Help them listen tonight at devotions and learn more about You. And please, help me not get so mad."

* * * * *

Judd joined Darin and Andrew at dinner but didn't eat much.

"You okay, Judd?" Darin asked. "I mean, is your stomach still messed up?"

"Not too bad," Judd answered. "I just don't want to move too fast."

"Well, all we have tonight is devotions, and then we'll go to bed. You'll probably be okay by tomorrow."

"Yeah."

Judd pulled a piece of his hotdog off and stuck it in his mouth. Seconds later, he clamped his hand over his mouth and leaned forward like he was going to hurl again. Darin and Andrew jumped up from their seats, spilling their plates in an effort to escape. All eyes in the building turned in their direction to see what was going on. "Just kidding!" Judd yelled, breaking into laughter. "Man! I had you guys!"

Andrew was turning purple, his hands doubled into fists at his sides, his face screwed into a furious frown. "Why, you ..."

Darin grabbed Andrew's arm and pulled him out the door of the screened-in dining hall. "Come on, Andrew. It isn't worth it."

"Just give me one punch," Andrew said, struggling to get away from Darin. "One punch, and I'll knock his lights out!"

"Having a problem, are we, boys?"

Darin looked up. It was Commander Stone.

"Darin and Andrew, right?"

They nodded. "It's nothing, sir," Darin said. "Andrew, here, just needed a breath of fresh air."

"Looks to me like Andrew can dish out pranks but can't take them himself. Isn't that about right, Andrew?" Commander Stone sunk to be eye-level with the boys. He took Andrew's arm and gently lifted his chin. "Look at me, Son."

Andrew looked up, and Darin noticed tears in his eyes.

"Had kind of a rough start, haven't we?" the commander asked. Andrew nodded. "What do you say we just start over, right here and now?"

"Start over?" Andrew asked, his voice squeaking ever so slightly. He cleared his throat. "What about K.P. duty?"

Commander Stone laughed. "We'll forget about that. I think maybe going to devotions might do you more good than scrubbing dishes and peeling potatoes for breakfast." He patted Andrew on the back and stood back up. "Now why don't you two go get another plate of food and gobble it down. You've got about five minutes before devotions, and breakfast is a long time away."

"Yes, sir," Darin and Andrew said in unison. "Thank you," Andrew added, sticking out his hand. The commander shook it heartily. "See you at the campfire."

Around the Campfire

"Are you glad to be at Camp Wilderness?" a short, round man with absolutely no hair shouted into the microphone that night at the campfire.

"Yes!" the boys returned.

"I can't HE-A-R you."

"YES!"

"Okay, that's more like it. Well... welcome to Camp Wilderness. My name is Commander Do-Right. I run the show around here, and my goal is to teach you about teamwork and how it will help you in your life."

"He looks like a human balloon with a belt around the middle," Andrew whispered to Darin. "Hope he's not full of hot air — we might lose him." A few campers nearby laughed.

"Oh, great. That's all Andrew needs — an audience."

"Sh-h," Darin said. "We're supposed to listen."

Andrew tightened his lips into a perfect circle, shut his eyes, put his hands together in front of his face, and started bowing slowly. "Yes, great master. Your wish is my command." More laughs from the crowd.

Darin tried to ignore him, concentrating, instead, on the speaker.

"Tonight we're kicking off our official 'Back to Nature Wilderness Weekend,' and before we go any further, we'd like to recognize those campers who wrote essays about teamwork in order to come.

"We? Has he got a frog in his pocket or something?" Andrew whispered.

Darin couldn't help but laugh. "Stop, Andrew."

"So," the speaker said. "We'd like the

winners of the essay contest to please stand at this time so we can give them a huge round of applause."

Cheers shot up as one-third of the campers jumped to their feet. Commander Do-Right stood at the front, clapping his hands in a circle the size of his rotund body — a round of applause. Andrew waited until the noise had almost died down to call out, "You go, DARIN!"

Darin felt the heat in his neck travel up to his ears. *"Thank God it is dark out... and... speaking of God... are You still there? I mean, I know You are, but I need some guidance here, Lord. On top of that, could You maybe put a muzzle on the boy next to me. He's about to get on my last nerve!"*

"Whoa!" Judd said. He was seated on the other side of Darin. "I want to learn how to do that!"

There was an older camper standing on the platform juggling fire sticks.

"Me, too," Darin answered.

"Not me," Andrew said, rubbing his chin. "I might singe my many facial hairs."

"Sick," someone behind him said. "Why don't you shut up and watch?"

Now it was Andrew's turn to go red.

"Thank you, Lord." Darin sighed in relief. Darin couldn't help but smile, though he put his hand up and pretended to yawn so Andrew wouldn't see it. Chewing his lip to keep a straight face, Darin reminded himself to listen. Commander Do-Right was talking about a competition the next day.

"Each team will be given everything it needs to survive one night in the wilderness — a pup tent, a compass, a flashlight, food, matches, and an emergency kit. Commander Stone is handing out the maps and emergency kits tonight so you can look them over. Each team will have its own site away from the others."

Someone at the end of the row handed Andrew a box of emergency kits and a stack of maps. He shoved them onto Darin's lap without a word. Darin took one of each and passed them on.

"Let's see where we're going to be," Judd said, yanking the map from Darin.

"Give it back, Judd," Andrew mumbled, reaching across Darin's lap and trying to grab the map back. "You know you can't read." Judd did not let go when Andrew pulled, and within seconds, they each had a piece of the map.

"Fine," Darin growled. "Now, look what you've done. We'll have to get another one."

But just as he said that, Commander Do-Right shouted, "Take care of your map. You only get one. If you lose it, you're out of the competition."

Darin took both pieces of the map and held them together. "We're in the middle. Looks like there's a creek just behind us. Maybe we'll even be able to fish."

Judd's eyes lit up. "This is like the neatest trip I've ever been on." Then he laughed. "Actually, it's the only trip I've ever been on."

Darin's stomach did a bit of a twist. "I'm glad I invited you, then," he told Judd. Andrew punched him in the leg as he said it, but even Andrew's sour mood couldn't touch the joy Darin felt watching Judd.

"So, you've never camped?"

"Are you kidding? I live in a camper! One big room for me, my little brother, and my parents. Makes our bunk house look like a castle!"

Andrew's jaw dropped. "You live in a camper? Far out! Do you like have a fire every night and roast marshmallows and tell scary stories and junk?"

Judd shook his head. "It's not like that. We live in this parking lot with about ten other families who are doing road construction. There's no campfire. There's not even any grass. Just a big garbage dumpster at the back of the lot. My brother and I mostly walk around and talk. When my dad doesn't have us pitching rock, that is."

Now Darin's stomach completely tied itself into a knot. He didn't know what to say. He didn't want to make Judd feel bad for the way he lived, but how could anyone live like that? He didn't have a bike to ride? A room of his own?

Andrew nudged Darin with his foot and rolled his eyes. Darin wasn't sure what to do now but gave in and rolled his eyes back. Then he turned to Judd to say... something.

But, what? He needn't have worried. Judd was already totally focused on the speaker again. A Commander Live-Right, he'd called himself. Darin forced himself to stop thinking about Judd and listen to the man up front.

"I'm here to bring you a short message from the Word of God," the commander said. "And I want to begin by telling you a story."

"Wake me up when it's over," Andrew whispered, leaning on Darin's shoulder and pretending to snore.

Darin shook him off and ignored him, never taking his eyes off the speaker.

"But before I begin, I need a volunteer..."

Judd Talks to Jesus

Campers everywhere jumped to their feet, screaming, "Me, me, me, me!"

The speaker looked out over the crowd and pointed. To Judd! "You! The one with the camouflaged jacket on. Come up here."

Darin couldn't believe it when Judd shook his head. He actually seemed shy and embarrassed. But the commander insisted, and soon, Commander Do-Right was at the end of their row of bleachers, reaching for Judd's arm. "Go, Judd," Darin called.

"Judd, Judd, Judd," the campers cheered.

With a grin the size of the Mississippi River on his face, Judd allowed himself to be led across the wooden stage and delivered to Commander Live-Right.

"Now, Son," the speaker said, taking Judd by the arm. "I need you to pretend to be a blind man.

"Dude," Judd said. "I can do it." The crowd laughed.

"Okay," the counselor said, tying a blindfold around Judd's head. "Your name is Bartimaeus."

"No!" Judd shouted out. "Anything but Bart!" Another laugh.

"Not Bart. Bartimaeus. You are a blind beggar who is sitting by the side of the road as Jesus was leaving the town of Jericho." The commander led Judd to the edge of the stage and pushed him gently into a sitting position.

"Couldn't I be Jesus and you be Bart?" Judd asked.

Now he had the commander laughing, too. "No. That won't work because I have to tell the story. I'll tell you when it's your turn to act. Just listen right now."

Bartimaeus nodded. "Yes, Jesus."

Darin was laughing so hard he thought he was going to wet his pants. Then he noticed that Andrew was laughing, too. Yes!

The commander continued. "Jesus had been teaching people in the town of Jericho how to live a Christian life. Folks there called him Rabbi — that means teacher."

"Hey, Rabbi," Bartimaeus called. "I'm not going to fall off this platform, am I? This isn't a trick or something, is it?"

"No, Bartimaeus. Hang on. I'm getting to your part." Turning back to the audience, the commander smiled and shook his head. Everyone laughed.

"What?" Bartimaeus hollered. The commander walked over and put his hand on his shoulder.

"Anyway, Jesus had finished teaching and was leaving the town when he passed by a blind beggar on the side of the road named ..."

"BARTIMAEUS!" the beggar shouted, curling his fingers into fists and pointing to his chest with his thumbs. "That would be ME!"

"Yes, it would at that," the speaker said. "And when this beggar heard that Jesus was passing by... "

"Better start walking, Jesus," Bartimaeus whispered loud enough for all to hear.

Jesus nodded and took a couple of steps. "The beggar called out to Jesus, saying, 'Jesus, Son of David, have mercy on me!'"

"Hey," Bartimaeus hollered, jumping to his feet. "That's my part." Stepping over to where he thought Jesus was standing, he cupped his hands and started to put them up to his mouth when he took that terrible step. Right off the platform!

"Judd!" Darin screamed.

But Commander Do-Right had seen it coming and had positioned himself on the ground just below Judd. Judd fell into his arms and practically bounced off his round little body to a standing position. Not a scratch on him anywhere. And he didn't miss a beat. Pulling the blindfold off just long enough to climb back on stage, he sat back down near the edge and called again. "Jesus, Son of David, have mercy on me!"

Commander Live-Right couldn't answer, he was laughing so hard.

"Yo! You there?" Bartimaeus called. "Don't let me down, Son of David. I need your mercy!"

The commander took a deep breath and put the microphone back up to his lips. "Well, Jesus heard the beggar calling and said, 'Call him over to me.' So they brought the beggar to Jesus ..."

"Pssst." Bartimaeus motioned with his hand over his mouth. "Could you come get me this time?"

"Sure," the Commander whispered back, outdone by roars of laughter from the campers. He walked over to Bartimaeus and helped him to his feet. "And Jesus said, 'Bartimaeus, what do you want me to do for you?'"

Bartimaeus grabbed the Commander's hand. "Hey, Jesus. I need some'o that miracle healing you been doing all over town! I want to see, Rabbi!"

"Go," the Commander said, removing the blindfold and placing his hands on Bartimaeus' eyes. "Your faith has healed you."

"Hallelujah!" Bartimaeus shouted, dancing around the platform. "I can see." Running back across the stage, he lifted the commander off his feet. "Give him a cheer everybody! The man totally rocks."

Everyone went wild, and Judd just stood there holding Commander Live-Right in the air until he asked Judd to put him down. Then, suddenly, Judd seemed to realize that all eyes in the place were on him, and instantly became embarrassed again. "Am I done?" he whispered to the commander.

"Yes," he answered. "Let's hear it for Judd! Great job!"

The campers jumped to their feet. "Go, Judd," they screamed until he had returned to his seat.

"Now," the speaker said. "I want to tell you that what Jesus did for Bartimaeus, He can still do for you and me. You may not be physically blind, and you may not have to beg for food, but you still need a miracle from God. You see, we've all been born spiritually blind and needy. God wants to open your spiritual eyes so you can see Him and hear His voice when He speaks to you. He wants to meet all your needs when you pray to Him. He wants to be your Lord and Savior. With God, all things are possible!"

Then the commander asked for those kids who had never invited Jesus into their hearts to come up to the platform and do so. Tons of kids went forward.

Darin kept his head bowed and his eyes shut. *"Please speak to Judd and Andrew, God. They need You so much. Especially Judd. Just knowing You would make his life so much better. Ple-e-ase, God. You know what to say to him in his heart. Let him hear You just like You let me hear You. Okay?"*

Darin opened his eyes. Judd and Andrew were still sitting on either side of him. He swallowed a lump in his throat. *"Well, maybe tomorrow night, God."*

Nothing is Impossible

Darin sneaked outside the next morning, before anyone else in the bunkhouse woke up. After making a trip to the toilet, he half-walked and half-slid down the wet, grassy slope to the lake. Cattails, wildflowers, and weeds swayed in the gentle breeze at the water's edge. A reddish glow spread across the lake, reflecting the rising sun just over the distant hills.

Crawling out onto the limb of a fallen tree, Darin sat above the water, breathing in the fresh mountain air, listening to baby birds squawking for their breakfast, and watching dragonflies buzzing across the surface of the water, stopping to rest every now and then.

"Ever wonder how the dragonflies are able to walk on water like that?"

Darin jumped and practically fell off the tree into the water.

"Whoa, there, partner." Commander Live-Right grabbed the back of Darin's sweatshirt until he regained his balance. "Didn't mean to startle you there."

"That's okay," Darin said. "I just didn't know anyone else was out here."

"Well, I'll leave you to your quiet time," the commander said, as he turned to leave. "Just wanted to say good morning."

Darin smiled. "Commander Live-Right?"

"Yes?" He paused at the edge of the water.

"Can I ask you a question?"

"Sure. Hang on. I'll come back out there."

Darin watched as the commander walked across the fallen tree, his arms to his sides for balance, and then dropped to a sitting position behind Darin.

"Wow! That was pretty cool."

"Took years of practice, Son. Been coming down here every spring for over ten years. Something about the early morning just draws me right into the presence of God."

Darin noticed the commander looking out over the lake as if he were all by himself out there. *Maybe I'm disturbing his quiet time.*

But in another second, the commander patted Darin's back. "Now, what's your question?"

"I... uh... I brought that kid, Judd, who was on the platform with you last night."

"Ah-h... Bartimaeus," he said with a smile. "Interesting young man."

"Very," Darin said. "Well, last night he told me that he lives in a camper. I mean, that's his house. Him and his little brother and their parents. They live in an old dirty parking lot with no grass or anything."

The commander shook his head. "His folks good to him?"

"I think so. I've seen his dad get pretty mad, but I've also seen him be pretty nice. Guess I don't really know for sure." Darin paused. "Thing is... I was wondering if maybe you could like pull him aside and tell him about Jesus and stuff... you know, like when he wouldn't be all embarrassed in front of the others."

Nodding, the commander rubbed his chin. "You ever talked to him about Jesus?"

Darin could feel his ears go red. "Uh, no, sir, not exactly. See... until yesterday, I only ever saw Judd at school and we don't really talk about that kind of... well, some of the kids don't like to talk about..."

"I understand." Commander Live-Right thought for a second. "I'll make you a deal. You go on your campout, and I'll pray that God will provide just the right moment for you to talk to Judd about Jesus. And if you don't get a chance, or he doesn't want to talk about it, you let me know Sunday morning and I'll find some time alone with him.

Darin grinned. "Thanks, sir. Judd really needs Jesus."

* * * * *

When breakfast was over, the campers met at the bleachers again. After saying the pledges and singing the national anthem and some other scout songs, the three commanders came to the platform.

"Hey, I wonder what Commander Roly-Poly is going to do," Andrew said when Commander Do-Right walked on stage with a lasso. "Hope there's nothing sharp up there that could pop his bubble!"

Andrew really was funny — even though he sometimes didn't know when to quit.

"Accept him, Darin. Just like Jesus has accepted you." Darin looked around. Here it was again. God talking straight to his heart. *"Andrew needs Jesus just as much as Judd does."* That peace that Darin had experienced in his bedroom a few weeks earlier was back. He knew God was there.

Shutting his eyes, he prayed silently. *"Is that You, God? I guess it is. I never thought about needing to accept Andrew, but I guess You're right. Duh — there I go again. Of course, You're right. I'll try to be more patient with Andrew. But I don't get how he could need Jesus as much as Judd. I mean, Judd lives in that camper and all..."* Darin's prayer was interrupted when Judd nudged him with his elbow.

"Do you think that's really Commander Do-Right?"

Darin cracked up laughing. Up on stage, the round, little commander sat on a bench playing a guitar. His hair was purple and spiked stiff with gel. He was wearing jeans with holes in them, ragged around the bottom, and a St. Louis Cardinals T-shirt.

Commander Stone stood at the microphone. "Did you all get enough for breakfast?"

The campers clapped.

"Well, I was so busy, I didn't get much time to eat. I'm sort of hungry. I wish I'd grabbed an apple from the fruit bowl to eat later." Hanging his head, he rubbed his stomach. "Man, I'm really hungry." Then, suddenly, he looked up, his eyes wide as saucers. "Hey! I just remembered. I have two pieces of bread in here somewhere." He dug around in his pants pockets and pulled out two crumbled slices of bread. "Yes!" he said, pumping his arm. The campers groaned. "This will be great," he continued, pressing the two pieces of bread

82

together and raising them to his lips. "But... I wish I had some peanut butter." He lowered the bread and looked at it for a second.

At this point, Commander Live-Right just happened to be walking by, his thumbs in his front pockets and his shoulders back. "You say peanut butter?"

"Well, yes," Commander Stone said. "For my sandwich, you know."

"I have some peanut butter on me."

"You do?"

Nodding, Commander Live-Right unbuttoned his shirt. His hairy belly was smeared with peanut butter.

"Gross!" the kids called. "Sick!"

But Commander Stone paid no attention. Slapping the bread to Commander Stone's belly, he smeared peanut butter all over the bread, pressed the bread together, and started to take a bite.

"No!" the audience screamed.

Commander Stone looked out at the audience. "No?"

"NO!"

He nodded. "Ah-h, you're right. I need some jelly." Turning slightly, he glanced over at Commander Do-Right who looked up from his guitar. "I, uh, don't suppose you have some jelly on you, do you?"

"Nope."

"Didn't figure you did." Again, he stuck the sandwich to his lips, but pulled it away again just before he took a bite. "I really need some jelly."

This time, Commander Do-Right jumped to his feet. "You know. Now that I think about it, I might have some jam!" And pulling off a shoe and sock, he stuck his foot up on the bench. "Toe Jam!"

Jelly was oozing from between his toes. Commander Stone curled his slices of bread and dipped them in the jelly, then mashed the bread back together again.

By now, the campers were hysterical — laughing and screaming. Some, practically heaving. Commander Stone took one last look at the sandwich and shook his head. "I guess I'm not so hungry after all."

The three commanders walked to the front and took a bow. The audience exploded with applause, and the commanders turned to leave the platform. But Commander Stone stopped just before he hit the steps and... you guessed it... took a huge bite of the sandwich AND swallowed it. Then he took another bite. And another. Until the sandwich was gone! Kids were rolling on the ground, they were laughing so hard.

When the campers finally started to settle down, Commander Live-Right returned to the microphone. "Now... the lesson to all of this." The kids got quiet. "I want you to know that when people are hungry, they'll eat just about anything. And there are a lot of kids out there who are hungry for friendship. For attention. Kids who are looking for someone to love them, and Jesus is who they're looking for.

"If they don't hear about Jesus, they might try drugs or alcohol. But those things won't make them happy. Only Jesus can save them from their sins and give them peace and joy. And it's your job to tell your friends the good news about a Friend who will never make fun of them or turn on them. A Friend who will change their lives. So, I challenge you Christian campers out there. Talk about Jesus around your campfires tonight. Let your lights shine!"

Let the Fun Begin!

When devotions were over, Commander Do-Right gave the campers some important training on wilderness camping and survival skills. Darin was amazed at how closely Judd and Andrew both listened. They really wanted to win this competition. Andrew and Judd had decided to let Darin choose the team name and he had opted for 'The God Squad.' It had a ring to it he thought and it might just keep the guys focussed on something other than the competition.

"And now," Commander Stone called,

returning to the microphone, "we're ready for the games. Are you ready to win?"

"Y-E-S-S-S-S!" they screamed.

"Okay. Choose one member of your team to run the 100 yard dash, and meet me at the track in about three minutes!"

Andrew jumped down from the bleachers. "You go, Darin. No one can beat you!"

"That's right," Judd agreed. "Unless you think I should try."

Andrew rolled his eyes. "I don't THINK so!"

"Just kidding," Judd said, grinning.

"Right," Andrew said. "Like I didn't know that."

"Huddle!" Darin said, pulling his friends into a circle. "Okay, guys. This is it. Do we want to win the gold medal?"

"Yes!" Judd and Andrew hollered.

"Then we've got to be a team. No more put downs and pranks. Got it?"

"Gottcha," Judd said.

Andrew looked at Judd for a second. "Okay," he said. "But don't think we're like all chummy or anything, Judd."

88

Nodding, Judd smiled. "I'm cool with that, Andrew."

"We have to come up with a name," Darin said. "How about God Squad?"

The others nodded and ran to the track, arriving just in time for Darin to stretch out a little before the race. He lined up with the other contestants.

"Piece of cake!" Andrew whispered hoarsely.

Darin ignored him, hoping no one else knew who Andrew was talking to. He concentrated on breathing and relaxing as he waited for the gun to go off.

"Three... Two... One... BANG!" The gun shot out and Darin took off in front. Halfway there, he was still in the lead, but two yards from the finish line, a red-headed kid to the left pulled out ahead and won the race."

"Good run," Darin said, shaking his hand.

Judd came up behind Darin and slugged him in the arm.

"Ow!" Darin cried — more surprised than hurt. "I hope there's an arm wrestling contest or something for you, Judd!"

"Let's go," Andrew said. "We're supposed to be over at the baseball diamond next. It's a batting contest. Can I go?"

"Sure," Darin said. Andrew was bound to get some points. He was the all-time best hitter for the entire fifth grade class.

Judd and Darin watched as Andrew hit three home-runs in a row to win first place in the competition. With hands in the air, he ran over to his team for high-fives. "We're ahead, so far! Next is the Tug-of-War."

"Yeah! That's got my name all over it," Judd said. He ran across the lot to where campers were already lining up. Commander Stone paired Judd up with another tall camper. "Good luck!" Judd called to his opponent.

"Shut your face!" the boy called back. "I don't need your best wishes. I'm going to shove your nose in the dirt."

Judd looked over at Darin and Andrew and mouthed the words, "What's up with him?" They shrugged their shoulders just as the gun rang out. Caught off guard, Judd immediately lost ground as the bully pulled him to the center.

"Go, Judd!" Andrew screamed. "You can do it!"

Judd planted his feet on the ground and tugged with all his might. The rope slipped through the bully's hands slightly. He lost his balance and let go for just a second.

"You ugly jerk!" he called. "I'll get you for that!" The bully grabbed the rope from the ground where Judd dragged him close to the center line.

Back and forth they went until finally, Judd's big toe slipped across the line and the judge announced that the bully was the winner. Judd stuck out his hand, but the bully brushed past him, shoving him with his shoulder.

"I'm not done with you, Bart!" he growled.

Judd balled his fingers into a fist and pulled his arm back. "Why, you..."

But Darin grabbed his arm just in time. "Shake it off, Judd. He's not worth it!"

"Yeah," Andrew added as the bully stomped away. "You're way better than him!"

"Go, Andrew," Darin thought, smiling. *"You're actually turning into a team player. Thanks, God. You've done it!"*

Darin came in first in the next game where he had to take his shoe off and balance it on his toes. Then he got three tries to stand behind a line and kick his shoe as far as possible. On his third try, he set a new camp record.

Andrew totally blew the next competition where he had to catch a water balloon in a dishtowel, coming in sixth.

Heading into the final competition, Darin's team was tied for first place with the bully's team. The campers headed into the activities building for the rock wall.

"Oh, no!" Andrew cried. "We'll never be able to do this!" He took a look at Judd. "No offense, Judd, but I can't see you hauling that" — he pointed to Judd — "up that" — he pointed to the wall. "Can you, Darin?"

"Not really. You want to try it, Andrew?"

"No way! I can't deal with heights."

"I can do this, guys," Judd insisted. "I promise!"

"NO!" Andrew screamed. "I'm sorry, Judd, but you want to win, don't you?"

"YES!" Judd screamed back. "And I know I can!"

Andrew rolled his eyes at Darin. Darin rolled them back and laughed. "Might as well let him try, Andrew. We can't do any better!"

Andrew shook his head. "I still think you have a better chance, Darin."

Judd looked at Darin, waiting for a decision. *"What do I do, God?"* Darin wasn't sure what to do. *"Well, I guess I'll go with Judd but, please, God, don't let Andrew blow a gasket if Judd loses again, okay?"*

"Go for it, Judd," Darin said, trying to sound confident.

"Yes!" Judd said, lining up to powder his hands.

The contest began. Judd grimaced as he pulled and stretched his body up the wall. By the time he reached the first level, half the kids had dropped out. Judd started the next level, still fighting to make it. The bully appeared next to him, laughing and sliding past Judd.

As Judd climbed onto the second ledge and grabbed a new rope for the final level, the bully sneered. "Eat my dust, Bart!"

"Hey, man," Judd said. "You need a major attitude adjustment!"

Bully didn't like that. He dropped his rope and headed in Judd's direction. Below, Darin and Andrew linked arms, and Darin prayed. Out loud! "God, help Judd. Protect him from that kid and help him to win."

"Amen!" Andrew added.

Fortunately, just as the bully reached Judd, an official showed up and told the boys to start climbing or they were going to be disqualified. And they were the only two going on!

So they began. Judd let the bully get started before he even took his first step.

"Go, Judd," Andrew screamed. "Don't give up!"

"Never!" Judd called back down. "With God, nothing is impossible. Watch this!" With that, he scooted up the last wall like it was nothing more than a slide at the park.

"YO!" Andrew screamed. "He was faking it!"

Judd zoomed to the top and rang the bell before Bully was even halfway up.

The God Squad had won the gold medal!

Setting Up Camp

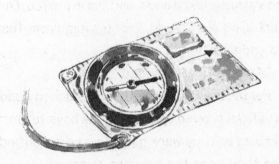

It was well into Saturday afternoon by the time the boys set out for their campsite. With Andrew manning the compass, they found the first two markers with no problem.

"One more," Judd said, "and we are on our own!"

Andrew nodded. "Sweet, isn't it?"

Arriving at camp, they unrolled their pup tent and spread the pieces out on the ground just like the commander had explained.

"You know how to do this, don't you?" Andrew asked Darin.

Darin rolled his eyes. "Actually?... No. My dad has always done it when we've gone camping. I usually just run to the lake and dive in."

"You're a big help."

"Here's the directions," Judd said. "I guess we can figure this out. After all, we're the gold medal campers, aren't we?"

"Yes!" Andrew and Darin said, throwing their hands in the air for a high five.

"Hey! Wait for me," Judd hollered, stepping up with his hand in the air. "I'm part of this team."

Darin laughed. "Yes, you are. A winning part!"

"Excuse me!" Andrew said, his hands on his hips. "Like I didn't hit three home runs in a row?"

"And like I didn't set a camp record for kicking my shoe off my foot?" Darin added. "You're right, Andrew. We couldn't have done it without each other."

"Guess that's what this team business is all about, huh?" Judd said. "Now, let's quit congratulating ourselves and get this tent set up before dark."

An hour later, as the sun began to disappear through the leaves, the boys had managed to prepare their camp — complete with a standing tent and a fire burning in the stoned-in circle provided. After ripping open the food container, they poked their hotdogs onto sticks Andrew had gathered and roasted their dinner.

"This is the life," Darin said, stretching out on the ground and leaning his head against a log he'd dragged near the fire. "Couldn't get better than this."

"Oh, I don't know," Judd said. "Might be a little better with these."

Darin and Andrew turned to see what Judd was talking about and found him holding up a huge handful of candy bars — at least fifteen of them.

"Whoa!" Andrew cried. "Where'd you get those?"

"My mom thought that she'd treat us since Darin's parents paid my way and all."

Sitting up, Darin took the Hershey Bar Judd handed him and opened it. "You rock, Judd!" Peeling off a square, he popped it into his mouth and grinned. "Sweet! I mean, this is really sweet!"

After stuffing themselves with candy bars and roasted marshmallows, Darin suggested they tell scary stories.

"Uh, I think it's creepy enough out here," Judd mumbled, looking around behind him. "I say we go in our tent and zip it up."

"You scared?" Andrew asked.

Judd didn't say he wasn't.

"Great. Here goes again, God. So much for being a winning team."

"You are scared, aren't you?" Andrew said. "There's nothing to worry about, Judd. I'll save you from the wild animals. Lions and tigers and bears, ha-ha. Lions and tigers and bears." He laughed.

"Stop it, Andrew," Darin said.

Judd headed for the tent.

"Aw, I'm just kidding, Judd. Come back out here," Andrew said. "We're not a team without you."

Judd stopped. "You mean it?"

Andrew stood and stuck out his hand. "Sure. You're turning out to be an okay guy now that you quit pulling all the stupid jokes and everything. In fact, you were a scream up there pretending to be Bart."

"Bartimaeus."

"Whatever. Anyway, I used to be afraid on camping trips, too. Until my dad taught me to really listen to the noises. Then I figured out that I was imagining most of what was freaking me out. Try it."

"Okay," Judd said, sitting back down.

"So..." Darin said. "Are we on with scary stories?"

"I've got a way better idea," Andrew said. "Let's find the bully's camp on the map and go sneak up on them. I can make a perfect coyote call. Listen." Andrew pursed his lips and shrieked into the night air. "Good, huh?"

Darin nodded. "Yeah, but I don't think we'd better leave camp."

Judd reached into his pocket. "We got any more matches?"

"Sure," Darin said. "Why?"

"We could use these on the bully." Judd held up three firecrackers.

"What did you bring those for, Judd?" Darin

asked, holding his head in his hands. "You're going to get us in trouble, for sure."

Andrew jumped up and walked over to Judd. "Awesome. Let's go. We can flush out the bully's camp"

Darin shook his head. "No way. That's really asking for trouble. Besides, the counselors will check on us around midnight. Remember?"

"Oh, come on, Darin," Andrew said. "Quit being such a church boy and have some fun."

"That hurt. Why did he have to say that? Why did I invite Andrew, anyway?"

"Shut-up, Andrew," Judd said. "What a dumb thing to say!"

"You joining the Jesus people, now, Judd?... Or should I say, Bartimaeus?"

"Whatever," Judd answered. "And yes, I am one of those Jesus people if that's what you want to call me."

Darin's eyes shot open — almost as wide as his mouth. "You are?"

Judd grinned and nodded. "Last night. When the commander called the kids forward? Well, I just prayed along in my mind. That counts, doesn't it?"

Darin laughed. "Yeah, of course. But why didn't you go forward?"

Hanging his head, Judd sighed. "Oh, I didn't want to like cause a scene or anything. If I'd gone forward, I probably would have tried to make something funny about it or something, and I didn't want to ruin it for everyone else."

"You did NOT pray that prayer," Andrew said, his eyes glued on Judd.

"Yes, I did. I was just doing it to see what would happen, but when I started praying, I guess I realized how bad I really am and how I need Jesus to take away my sins."

"Did you hear Him talk to you or something?" Andrew asked. "Cause if you tell me you did, I'm gonna really think you're nuts."

"No," Judd said. "I didn't hear voices or anything weird. I just got this feeling everything was going to be okay. All of a sudden it was like I was getting a whole new try at living. You should give it a try, Andrew."

"That's NOT going to happen."

"It's cool," Judd continued. "I don't have to keep beating myself up for being such a nerd.

Now that I have Jesus living on the inside of me, life is way too awesome."

"Whatever," Andrew said. "Anyway, let's get the matches and head for the bully's camp."

"Don't do it, Judd," Darin pleaded.

"Aw, come on," Judd said. "It won't hurt anything. I'll just throw them somewhere in the distance. We just want to see the dudes jump!"

"Yes!" Andrew shouted, throwing Judd a high-five. "Come on, Darin. We're a team, and you're outnumbered. Besides, we might get lost without you. We won't go to the Bully's camp - one of the other ones will be just as much fun. You know you want to..."

Darin stood. He knew this must be one of those moments where he was being asked to make the right choice or the wrong choice.

"Well, let me get the flashlight to read the map."

Andrew Takes an Extra Trip

The boys banked their fire and started off, looking for the markers listed on the map. From the looks of it, the bully's camp was only a couple of camp sites away — through the trees and to the left. It was pretty dark and kind of scary but the boys felt brave enough to do anything. They were tough guys after all.

"Here," Darin said, handing Andrew the flashlight as they tramped through the woods. "Hold this so I can see the map."

Andrew grabbed the flashlight and tried to help Darin interpret the map. But, not watching where he was walking, Andrew tripped over a tree root and went sprawling down a hill on the side of the path. The flashlight flew from his hands, hit a tree trunk, and shattered — leaving the boys in pitch dark.

"NO!" Judd gasped, an edge of pure terror creeping into his voice. "Darin, where are you? Let's get out of here! DARIN!" Judd was beginning to scream now.

Darin thumped around in the dark for Judd's arm. "STOP, JUDD," he yelled. His screaming was getting a bit much now. "You're going to be fine. We've got to help Andrew."

"NO!" Judd hollered again. "You're not going anywhere. Stay with me, Darin. I'm creeped to the max!"

"Darin!" Andrew called. "I can't walk. I think I've broken my ankle."

"Oh, God, what should I do? Are You here with us? That's the answer. Of course God is with us."

"Judd," Darin said. "You said you asked Jesus into your heart, right?"

Judd nodded, hanging on to Darin's arm with a death grip.

"Okay, then," Darin said, prying Judd's fingers off, one at a time. "Start acting like it. God is right here with you. He won't let anything hurt you."

"Here?" Judd asked, looking around suspiciously. "What's He doing here?"

"DARIN!" Andrew called. "Quit preaching and come help me, would you?"

"I'm coming," Darin hollered. "There's a verse in the Bible that says God will never leave us nor forsake us, Judd. Now, just keep saying that over and over while I go down and help Andrew. Got it?"

Judd grabbed a tree nearby. "I'll try."

As his eyes adjusted to the dark, Darin felt for the next tree and slowly made his way down the slope, thankful to see that Andrew had only fallen a few yards.

"Can you stand?" he asked, trying to get a grip under Andrew's arms.

"I think so. On my right foot."

As Darin pulled, Andrew rose to his feet — or, to his foot, actually. He tried to hop a step up the slope, but lost his balance and tumbled back to the ground, taking Darin with him. Half-laughing and half-crying, Darin tried to stand. "You're on my foot, Andrew. Get off my foot."

"Darin? Andrew?" It was Judd. "You guys okay?"

"We're super, Judd," Andrew said, laughing. "How about you?"

"Stop, Andrew," Darin said. "Let's try again." It didn't work. Andrew couldn't do it. Darin tried dragging Andrew, but he was way too heavy. "Judd?"

"Yeah?"

"You're going to have to come down here and help me lift Andrew."

"No way, Jose!"

"I mean it, Judd. We're a team, remember?"

"Right. I'll be a team in the daytime, but I am definitely not coming down there in the dark. It is NOT going to happen!"

"Fine, Judd. Just leave us down here, then," Andrew said. "And I thought you said that with God, nothing was impossible."

"Nope," Judd said. "That was the Rabbi that said that."

Darin sighed. *"Okay, God. What next?"*

"Darin?" Andrew whispered.

"Yeah?"

"I think a snake just slid across my arm. Don't scream. Can you see anything?"

Darin freaked. "I am SO out of here, Andrew. Let's go!" Darin started climbing up the slope. "Come on, Andrew. You've got to try."

"Andrew needs help. You know that. Remember how Jesus suffered for you?"

Great. What a time for God to remind him of that! Turning around, Darin slid back down the slope. "You okay?"

Andrew laughed. "Yeah. I moved my arm very slowly and realized it was just a branch. Had me scared for a minute there."

Darin shook his head. "JUDD! GET DOWN HERE, RIGHT NOW!

"What?"

"NOW! I MEAN IT!

"Yeah," Andrew added. "You get down here or I'm going to tell everyone at school

107

that you're afraid of the dark! And I'm not kidding!"

"You wouldn't!"

"Try me!"

"Okay, I'm coming."

In a few minutes, Darin saw Judd coming — in a sitting position. "Over here."

Judd arrived, picked Andrew up, and tucked him under his arm like a football. "Lead the way, Darin. I ain't hanging around here for a party or anything."

Anybody Seen the Batteries?

Judd and Darin managed to get Andrew back to the campsite and settled in front of the fire. Darin lifted Andrew's pants leg to have a closer look at his ankle.

"Whoa! This is already super swollen!"

Andrew moaned and nodded slightly, his head resting on a pillow Judd had gotten from the tent. "It hurts something awful, Darin!"

Darin looked at his watch. "And it's only nine o'clock. This can't wait until midnight. We've got to get you some help." Darin thought for a minute. "Bring me the emergency kit from the tent, Judd."

"No, Darin," Andrew said. "We'll lose major points if we break the seal on anything in that kit.I don't think it's a good idea."

"I don't care what you think," Darin said as Judd handed him the black box and he opened the lid.Commander Do-Right told us to use this walkie-talkie if we had an emergency."

"Yeah," Judd said. "And he also said that we'd lose the points regardless of our excuse."

"Okay," Darin said. "So winning isn't everything.We got the gold medal today.So what if we don't get the one for tomorrow."

Judd nodded. "You're right.I say we call."

"NO!" Andrew said. "Please."

But Darin didn't listen.He ripped the paper cover from the walkie-talkie. "Look," he said. "This thing was already torn open.Someone didn't rewrap it from the last camp.We couldn't have won, anyway."

"That stinks," Judd said. "We should have checked it before we left."

"Darin?" Andrew said.

"Not now, Andrew," Judd answered. "I'm calling the camp. We need to get some ice for that ankle. I'll bet they'll take you to some emergency room nearby."

"Darin?" Andrew said, a little louder.

Ignoring Andrew, Darin pushed the power button for the third time. Nothing happened. "Great. The batteries are dead."

"Maybe they're just in backwards," Judd suggested.

"Darin?"

"What, Andrew?" Darin said, flipping the lid off the battery compartment. "NO WAY!" he shouted. "There aren't any batteries in this thing!"

"DARIN!" Andrew hollered. "That's what I've been trying to tell you, if you'll listen to me. I broke the seal last night and used the battery in my video game after you guys went to sleep."

"You WHAT?" Darin asked. "You didn't just say what I thought you said?"

Andrew nodded. "Sorry."

"So where's the video game?" Judd asked. "In your backpack?"

Andrew shook his head. "I had to hide it under my bunk last night when the counselor came by. And I forgot to get it this afternoon."

"So...it's still back at camp?" Judd asked.

"With the batteries?" Darin added.

Andrew nodded. "Guess I messed up, huh?"

"BIG TIME!" Judd and Darin answered at the same time.

"We're stuck out here in the dark with no flashlight and no walkie-talkie."

"I know - but who was it that decided fire-crackers was a good idea, and who showed us how to get to the camp?"

"So what - who went and fell on his face and broke his ankle and made sure we have no chance of winning now."

All three boys were soon yelling at each other and the campsite was far from peaceful... until Darin muttered, "This sure isn't teamwork." To himself he whispered, *"This sure isn't honoring God. Jesus doesn't want me going off like this. No sir."* He whispered the Bible verse from Romans: 'May the God who gives endurance and encouragement give you a spirit of unity among yourselves as you follow Christ Jesus, so that with one heart and mouth you may glorify the God and Father of our Lord Jesus Christ. Accept one another, then, just as Christ accepted you, in order to bring praise to God.'

The camp site was quiet for several minutes except for the crackle of the flames and an occasional moan from Andrew.

"Okay," Darin said, finally. It was time to get back on track. "Let's think about our survival training. What was it Commander Do-Right said for us to remember?"

"S.T.O.P.," Judd said. "Stop, Think, Observe, and stay Put.

Darin looked over at Andrew's ankle. It was turning black and blue and had swollen even more. "Andrew's going to have to stay put, but one of us has to go for help."

Judd's eyes grew as big as the yolk in the sunnyside-up egg Darin had eaten for breakfast. "Alone? Like without a flashlight or anything?"

Darin nodded. "Unless you have a better idea."

"Why don't you go together?" Andrew suggested. "Leave me here. I'll be fine."

"No way," Darin said.

"Like what's anyone going to do for me, anyway?" Andrew pointed out. "I'll be safe inside the tent. What if one of you - - -"

"Definitely not me!" Judd said.

"Shut up, Judd," Darin said. "Go ahead, Andrew."

"What if one of you tries to go get help and hurts yourself? Who's going to know? It's just not smart to take off by yourself."

"You're right," Darin admitted. "We'll memorize the route to the next camp site so we can get there in the dark. If something happens to us, you can show our route to the counselor when he gets here. How's that sound?"

"Perfect," Andrew said.

"Uh, except for one thing," Judd said. "I am NOT going back out there in the dark."

Darin stood. "Oh, yes, you are, Judd Becker, because I KNOW you do not want your father to find out you refused to help a friend in need!"

"Aw, come on, Darin," Judd said. "Have a heart."

"My heart is just about worn out. Now my head is kicking in, and I'm not going to take no for an answer. Got it?"

"Okay, okay. Just don't get so hyper!"

Darin and Judd memorized the route, drawing it over and over in the dirt with sticks until they could see it in their minds. Then they helped Andrew into the tent and made sure the fire was safely contained. But just as they started off, Andrew called them back.

"Uh, Darin?"

"Yeah? Don't tell me you're scared, now, Andrew."

"Well, yes, a little. But I'll be okay. I just thought maybe you might want to do that prayer thing again. It seemed to work pretty good earlier today."

Darin smiled and prayed and then he and Judd set off into the darkness of the night.

No Help From The Bully

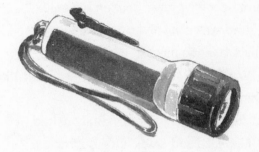

It took Darin and Judd only about ten minutes to find another campsite. But it wasn't the one they set out for. Somehow, they'd gotten turned around and ended up at the bully's camp.

"Great," Darin mumbled under his breath as they stumbled into the campsite. "How did we do this?"

"I'm not sure," Judd mumbled back, "but Bully doesn't look too happy."

Bully was seated by the campfire with two other boys, all three as big or bigger than Judd.

"So, what are you doing here, Bart?" Bully asked. "Lose your vision?"

"You might say that."

"Actually," Darin said, "our flashlight broke and one of our team fell and hurt himself. We think he might have broken his ankle."

"And we're involved in what way?" one of Bully's friends asked.

"We'd like to borrow your walkie-talkie," Darin said.

"You broke that, too?" Bully asked.

"Nope," Judd said. "Our batteries..."

"Our batteries aren't working for us," Darin interrupted. "So, can we use yours?"

"Our batteries?" Bully asked, slapping his friend on the knee.

"Good one," his friend said, laughing.

Darin shifted about while he waited for their attention. Finally, they looked his way. "Please, could we use your walkie-talkies?"

The boys looked to Bully. He shook his head. "Ain't gonna happen. We're not losing points just cause you messed up."

"What about your flashlight, then?" Darin asked. "We just need it long enough to get back to camp, then we'll bring it back to you. Come on, guys.Our friend's hurting!"

One of Bully's friends crawled inside their tent and came out with the flashlight. "Here," he said, handing it to Darin. "Your friend okay by himself over there?"

"I think so," Darin said. "I don't want to take time to go back that way.I'd rather hurry back to camp to get the medic."

"Hey!" Bully said. "Who's the captain of this team, anyway?"

"You are," the kid said. "But not loaning them the flashlight is just wrong."

"Thanks," Darin said as he and Judd walked off in through the woods.

* * * * *

Judd and Darin hitched a ride back to their campsite on the medic's golf cart. After examining Andrew's ankle, the medic announced it was seriously sprained, but not broken.He gave Andrew some pain medicine to help him relax and loaded him onto the cart.At Darin's request, the medic promised to return the flashlight to the other campsite.

When the golf cart had driven away, Judd and Darin put out their fire and climbed inside their tent.

"Big night, huh?" Darin said.

"Yeah," Judd answered. "You ready to go to sleep?"

"In just a little bit. I wanted to ask you about something first, Judd."

"Me?"

"Yeah. You said you asked Jesus into your heart. Did you mean it? I mean, like forever?"

"I guess."

"Because it's not like something you do just for camp. It's a lifetime thing."

"I know."

"I'm really glad you came, Judd. Think you might want to come with me to church on Sundays and Youth Group on Wednesday nights?"

"Sure, if my parents will let me."

"Good."

The Awards Ceremony

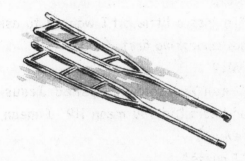

As they sat in the bleachers on Sunday morning, waiting for the ceremony to begin, Andrew turned to Judd.

"Thanks for being willing to come down the hill and carry me up, last night, Judd," Andrew said.

Judd blushed. "Like I had a choice."

"True," Andrew said. "But it still took a lot of courage."

Commander Do-Right stepped up to the microphone. "And now, to wrap up Camp Wilderness for another year, we'd like to announce our top three winners."

Darin fidgeted with the edge of his seat as the commander announced the bronze and silver winners and awarded their medals to them.

Word had gotten around that the bully's team had been eliminated because of their unwillingness to loan their walkie-talkies to a fellow camper in need.Commander Live-Right had talked all about the price of friendship and how much more important that should be than simply winning a contest.He didn't actually mention the bully's team or anything, but everybody knew.Darin had sneaked a glance at them one time during devotions only to receive a snarl from the bully himself.

"This is us!" Judd whispered, grabbing Darin's leg. "I can't believe it!"

"And now..." the commander was saying... "I'd like to present the second gold medal to the God Squad! Let's give them a giant round of applause as they come forward for their awards."

Darin, Judd, and Andrew — proudly hopping on crutches — made their way to the front and up the steps to the platform.All the campers stood and cheered.Well, almost all of them.

One stayed seated and actually called out a boo until Commander Stone got hold of him.

Darin had that warm feeling again. *"You've brought honor to God's name."* Darin knew that honoring God was better than any gold medal he could ever win.He smiled as Commander Do-Right hung the medal around his neck. *"Thanks for Your help, God,"* Darin breathed a prayer. *"Thanks for helping me."*

When they'd all three received their awards, the commander asked if they had anything to say.Andrew and Judd declined immediately, but Darin stepped forward.

"I just want to say thanks to Andrew and Judd who are not only my team members but also two of my best friends."

Everyone clapped again as the boys headed back to the bleachers.

"Hey, Darin," Judd said. "Don't take that medal to school for show and tell. Never know what might happen to it."

Darin laughed. "Thanks for the advice friend!"

The Purple Heart

Barbara Haley

Darin's Dad is a war hero with the medal to prove it! Darin wants to show his father's Purple-Heart Medal to the rest of the class but his father will not allow it out of his sight.

However, when Darin takes it anyway this leads to a whole lot of trouble. The medal goes missing and Darin sets out to prove who the culprit is. It's bound to be that horrible new boy in the class - he dresses weird and is nasty to all the other kids. But in this nail biting, hilarious story, there is an incredible twist at the end - and everybody learns about the value of truth and the danger of lies.

1 85792 920 9

Goal Behind the Curtain

Cliff Rennie

Doug Mackay has been spotted by the manager of Dalkirk Albion - and not without reason. He's a first class football player.

It's not long before Doug is on the team for the European championship! Their first match is scheduled for Czechoslovakia. Doug, a committed Christian, agrees to smuggle some Bibles into Eastern Europe.

With Dalkirk Albion's continued success through the championships Doug continues his dangerous exploits in Bible smuggling. But the biggest threat seems to be coming from his own team.

1 87167 647 9

Offside in Ecuatina

Cliff Rennie

It's Scotland against England at Wembley. The Scotland manager is looking for some fresh energy. His eyes fall on the young Dalkirk Albion star, Doug Mackay.

Doug's performance on the field is first class and wins him a place in the squad for the world cup in Ecuatina but in the dangerous back streets of the South American capital, Doug uncovers a plot to overthrow the President.

1 87167 669 X

THE BIG GREEN TREE AT NO. 11
Tammy and Jake learn about Life and Death
Catherine Mackenzie

Tammy and Jake live at Number 11. Canterbury Place with their mum and dad and the family dog. Through different situations they sensitively discover about life and death and the God who loves them.

1 85792 731 1

Staying faithful – Reaching out!

Christian Focus Publications publishes books for adults and children under its three main imprints: Christian Focus, Mentor and Christian Heritage. Our books reflect that God's word is reliable and Jesus is the way to know him, and live for ever with him.

Our children's publication list includes a Sunday school curriculum that covers pre-school to early teens; puzzle and activity books. We also publish personal and family devotional titles, biographies and inspirational stories that children will love.

If you are looking for quality Bible teaching for children then we have an excellent range of Bible story and age specific theological books.

From pre-school to teenage fiction, we have it covered!

Find us at our web page: www. christianfocus.com